For my little Junoberry – L.F.

First published in Great Britain in 2013 by
Piccadilly Press Ltd, 5 Castle Road, London NW1 8PR
www.piccadillypress.co.uk

Text and illustrations copyright © Lorna Freytag, 2013

Designed by Simon Davis
Colour reproduction by Dot Gradations
Printed and bound in China by WKT

ISBN: 978 1 84812 314 4 (h/b)
ISBN: 978 1 84812 313 7 (p/b)

1 3 5 7 9 10 8 6 4 2

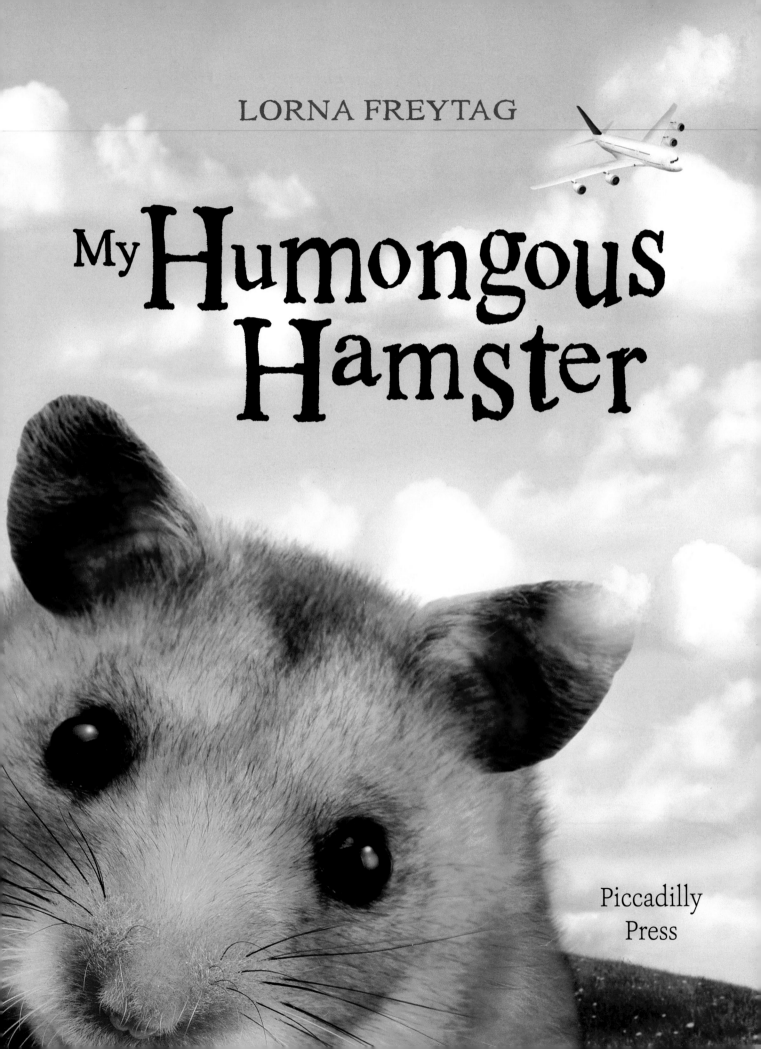

LORNA FREYTAG

My Humongous Hamster

Piccadilly
Press

My hamster doesn't do much.
He just sleeps and eats and eats and sleeps.

Sometimes he gets so
HUMONGOUSLY HUNGRY
that I think he might eat his whole
bowl of food in one huge gulp.
If he does that, he will get

BIGGER
and
BIGGER.

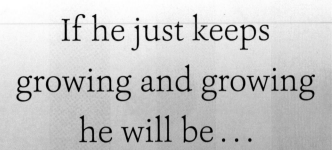

If he just keeps
growing and growing
he will be . . .

. . . ENORMOUS!

He wouldn't fit into his
cage any more,
or my bedroom.

He would have
to go outside.

He'd eat trees like broccoli.

He'd be a danger
crossing
the road.

But he'd have a lot of fun at the fair.

And he'd be able
to see for
MILES!

He could give me and my

friends a lift to the park.

He
might
even
help
the
police
catch
CRIMINALS,

or rescue someone
in trouble.

The neighbour's cat
wouldn't like him...

...or next door's dog!

In fact, I think I'd find
him scary myself,

especially if he got
ANGRY.

And would he sleep …

… under a bridge?

… in a circus tent?

… at the foot of a mountain?

… or in someone else's house?

I'm sure he'd miss us playing together.

So I think he would
be glad to shrink back
to normal hamster
size again,

and be ready for
another hamster sleep,
in his usual
hamster house …

…until
the next
time
he gets

HUMONGOUSLY

HUNGRY!!